I Remember Miss Perry

Pat Brisson

illustrated by Stéphane Jorisch

Dial Books for Young Readers

For dedicated teachers everywhere,
especially my good friend Linda Reuter,
who requested this story from me
—P.B.

To Terry Wong, my friend in grade three
—S.J.

DIAL BOOKS FOR YOUNG READERS • A division of Penguin Young Readers Group • Published by The Penguin Group • Penguin Group (USA) Inc., 375 Hudson Street, New York, NY 10014, U.S.A. • Penguin Group (Canada), 90 Eglinton Avenue East, Suite 700, Toronto, Ontario, Canada M4P 2Y3 (a division of Pearson Penguin Canada Inc.) • Penguin Books Ltd, 80 Strand, London WC2R 0RL, England • Penguin Ireland, 25 St. Stephen's Green, Dublin 2, Ireland (a division of Penguin Books Ltd) • Penguin Group (Australia), 250 Camberwell Road, Camberwell, Victoria 3124, Australia (a division of Pearson Australia Group Pty Ltd) • Penguin Books India Pvt Ltd, 11 Community Centre, Panchsheel Park, New Delhi-110 017, India • Penguin Group (NZ), Cnr Airborne and Rosedale Roads, Albany, Auckland 1310, New Zealand (a division of Pearson New Zealand Ltd) • Penguin Books (South Africa) (Pty) Ltd, 24 Sturdee Avenue, Rosebank, Johannesburg 2196, South Africa • Penguin Books Ltd, Registered Offices: 80 Strand, London WC2R 0RL, England

Designed by Teresa Kietlinski
Text set in Excelsior
Manufactured in China on acid-free paper

1 3 5 7 9 10 8 6 4 2

Library of Congress Cataloging-in-Publication Data
Brisson, Pat.
I remember Miss Perry / Pat Brisson ; illustrated by Stéphane Jorisch.
p.   cm.
Summary: When his teacher, Miss Perry, is killed in a car accident, Stevie and his elementary school classmates take turns sharing memories of her, especially her fondest wish for each day.
ISBN 0-8037-2981-2
[1. Teachers—Fiction. 2. Death—Fiction. 3. Grief—Fiction. 4. Schools—Fiction.] I. Jorisch, Stéphane, ill. II. Title.
PZ7.B78046Ir 2006   [E]—dc22   2004024070

The art was created with pen and ink, watercolor, and gouache.

When my dad got a new job, we had to move. It was scary starting a new school where all the other kids already had best friends. I told my mom how afraid I was.

"I don't know anybody! Who will I talk to at lunch?"

My mother gave me a hug. "First days are hard," she said, "but I'm sure you'll do fine, Stevie. Just be friendly."

I tried being friendly, but the closer to lunchtime it got, the more my stomach hurt. It hurt so much when the lunch bell finally rang that I told my teacher I had to go to the nurse.

Miss Perry said, "Oh, Stevie, I'm sorry you don't feel well. I know what it's like to be the new person. I was the new teacher here this year and my stomach hurt the first day too."

"It did?" I said. "I didn't know teachers got stomachaches."

Miss Perry's eyes almost disappeared when she smiled. "Oh, sure," she said. "Anything that happens to anyone else can happen to a teacher too."

Thinking about Miss Perry with a stomachache made mine hurt a lot less. And it stopped hurting altogether when she said, "It is my fondest wish that you join me for lunch today, Stevie."

The way Miss Perry said "fondest wish" made me feel like I was talking to a princess in a fairy tale.

So I ate lunch with Miss Perry that day, but every day after that, I ate with my new friend, Josh. I didn't get any more stomachaches for a long time.

I soon found out that Miss Perry had a new fondest wish every day. One day her fondest wish was for everyone to quiet down quickly so she could read us a chapter of *James and the Giant Peach.*

Another day her fondest wish was that Dylan and Jonathan would stop bugging each other. Another time her fondest wish was for all of us to plant daffodil bulbs around the flagpole in front of school.

Once, while we were learning all about honeybees,
Miss Perry said, "Class, today is Mrs. O'Brien's birthday."

"How old is she?" Josh asked.

Miss Perry smiled at him. "Old enough to be a great principal!" she said. "And it is my fondest wish that we buzz down to her office and sing her the birthday song."

Of course, we all agreed. We made bee costumes out of
trash bags and construction paper. We practiced singing
"Happy Birthday" by buzzing instead of using the words.

Then we all flew down the hall to the office.

"Buzz–buzz buzz–buzz buzz buzzzzz! Buzz–buzz buzz–buzz buzz buzzzzz!"

Miss Perry said, "I've brought you a swarm of well-wishers,
Mrs. O'Brien!"

Our principal was so surprised, she stopped her work just so
she could listen to us. When we finished singing, she thanked us
and said, "This is definitely the buzziest birthday I've ever had."

Miss Perry smiled until her eyes disappeared.

One day in March, Miss Perry didn't come to school. Mrs. O'Brien came to our class instead and got us started doing some math problems. But people kept coming to the door and Mrs. O'Brien would have to stop doing math to go talk to them.

After lunch that day, we went back to our classroom and were surprised to find our parents there. Some were squeezed into kids' desks. Others were standing by the windows.

Mrs. O'Brien said, "Girls and boys, I have something very sad to tell you. It's so sad that I wanted your parents to be here with you when you heard it."

We looked at our parents' faces. They looked sad too.

Mrs. O'Brien said, "Miss Perry was in a car accident this morning on the way to school. A car that was coming the other way crossed over the line in the middle of the road and hit Miss Perry's car." Mrs. O'Brien's eyes filled up with tears and she took a deep breath. "I'm so sorry, boys and girls," she said. "Miss Perry died in the accident."

Nobody said a word. Some kids buried their faces in their parents' sides. A few started crying. Finally, Dylan asked, "Is that why she wasn't in school today?"

"Yes, Dylan," Mrs. O'Brien told him, "that's why."

"Will she be back to school tomorrow?" Jonathan asked.

"No, Jonathan, I'm sorry. Miss Perry won't be back to school," Mrs. O'Brien said.

"Will we ever see her again?" I asked.

But Mrs. O'Brien started crying and could only shake her head. No.

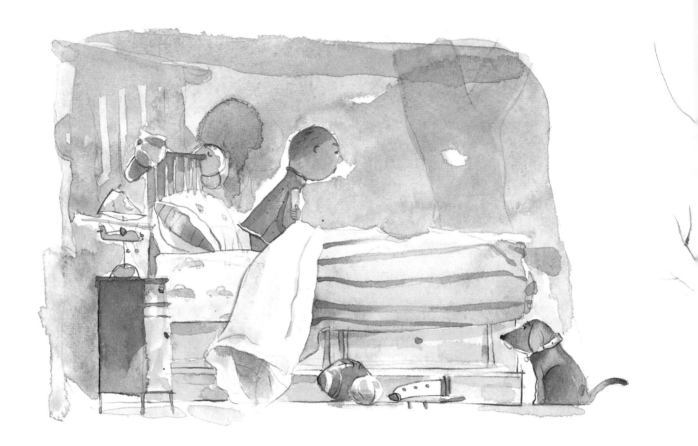

I got a stomachache that night and I didn't
want to go to school the next day. It felt like
the first day all over again. Only now it was
the first day without Miss Perry.

Mrs. O'Brien was with our class that whole day. Ms. Jackson, the counselor, was with us too. She told us, "It's okay to cry when someone you like very much has died." She gave each of us a packet of tissues and said, "If tears surprise you during the day, you'll be ready for them." I wondered if one packet of tissues would be enough.

Then Ms. Jackson asked us to tell her about Miss Perry.

At first nobody said anything. Then Mrs. O'Brien told how we had all dressed up like bees to wish her a happy birthday. "And we sang 'Happy Birthday' with buzzes instead of words," Josh told Ms. Jackson. We smiled, remembering.

Little by little, we told Ms. Jackson more things about Miss Perry. We told her about the stories she read to us, the plays she helped us perform, the songs we sang, the art projects we made, the walks we took.

"Remember when Miss Perry's fondest wish was that we all memorize a poem every day for a week?" Cheryl asked.

"And the time her fondest wish was that we all learn to square dance!" Lydia said.

Ms. Jackson looked confused. "Her 'fondest wish'?" she asked. "What do you mean?"

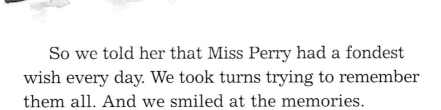

So we told her that Miss Perry had a fondest
wish every day. We took turns trying to remember
them all. And we smiled at the memories.

"When Miss Perry told us her fondest wish every day," I said, "it was almost like she was a princess in a fairy tale!"

I remembered my first day in Miss Perry's class and how she had turned it from a bad day to a good one for me.

Ms. Jackson smiled at us. "And what do you think would be Miss Perry's fondest wish today?" she asked.

We got quiet then, because we knew we wouldn't be hearing Miss Perry's fondest wish ever again. Some of the kids cried. Some put their heads down on their desks.

At last Cheryl said, "I think her fondest wish would be for us to not be too sad."

"And to remember the fun things we did together," Lydia said.

"To always get along with each other," said Jonathan. Dylan nodded his head in agreement.

"To learn a lot in school," said Josh.

"But most of all," I said, "to be happy, like she was
always happy," and I remembered Miss Perry,
and how her eyes disappeared when she smiled.